A Respectable Occupation

JULIA KERNINON

A Respectable Occupation

Translated
from the French
by Ruth Diver

LesFugitives

• This first English-language edition published in Great Britain in July 2020 by Les Fugitives • 91 Cholmley Gardens, Fortune Green Road, London NW6 1UN • www.lesfugitives.com • Originally published as *Une activité respectable* © Rouergue, 2017 • English-language translation © Ruth Diver 2020 • Foreword © Lauren Elkin 2020 • Cover design by Dominic Lee © Les Fugitives 2020 • Front cover photograph of Julia Kerninon © Renaud Monfourny • All rights reserved • A CIP catalogue record for this book is available from the British Library • The rights of Julia Kerninon and Ruth Diver to be identified respectively as author and translator of this work have been identified in accordance with Section 77 of the Copyright, Designs and Patents Act 1988 • Typesetting by Charles Boyle • Printed in England by TJ International Ltd, Padstow, Cornwall • The Publisher acknowledges financial assistance from the Institut français (Paris) as part of their programme of aid to publication, as well as from Arts Council England.

• ISBN 978-1-9993318-1-8 •

Foreword by Lauren Elkin

vii

A Respectable Occupation

1

Foreword

In the end, it is difficult to say where reading ends and writing begins. It is one coextensive gesture: breathe in words, breathe out words. Inspiration comes from Latin; it means to inhale. Take in one story, emit another; you've shifted the form of the book. When you exhale on the page, it's in your own unique element.

The greatest writers are also the greatest readers. Virginia Woolf, Roland Barthes, Jeanette Winterson – they all read, as Woolf put it, 'to refresh and exercise [their] own creative powers.' They can't stop themselves from writing about reading. They have origin stories of how reading and writing became as necessary as breathing.

Julia Kerninon's *A Respectable Occupation* joins the shelf of these biblioautobiographies: books on how writers crave books, how books beget books, how tricky it is to move from the position of the reader to that of the writer and stand there feeling you've earned the right to call yourself, finally, a *writer*.

Her origin story begins, as so many do, at *Shakespeare and Company* in Paris. On a trip to the capital from their home in the provinces, Kerninon and her mother in matching fake leopard fur coats visit the famous bookshop, which took up an oversized place in her childhood cartography of 'places that mattered,' 'place[s] we *belonged* to.' A drawing of the bookshop hangs on the wall,

> like a family property we might have owned [...] I felt relieved to be able to trail my hand along the shelves and assure myself at last they were real. [...] I had found my way back to the vessel that had brought me into the world.

Reading, for Kerninon, is a physical need, inherited in the blood. Once, in Nebraska, her mother came across a battered thing in a ditch, and, moving with the intuition of a drug addict in withdrawal, she crawled on her stomach through the frosty grass to get hold of what was, indeed, a book.

This is an image in which we bibliomaniacs can easily recognise ourselves, those of us who are desperate enough for the printed word to read literally whatever is at hand – romance novels in a B&B, an abandoned newspaper on the metro, the ingredients on the labels of cleaning products while on the loo.

Books saved Kerninon's mother – and so many others – from 'a hopeless childhood,' and the love of reading she bequeathed to her daughter is a gift but also a potlatch, 'an immeasurably generous offering, which I might be expected to return one day with an even greater gift.' In the early chapters of *A Respectable Occupation*, Kerninon's mother oversees her daughter's progress, making sure she's actually using her typewriter ('You need to get to work, because that's what writers do, they work, you know'). Skipping around in time – now in deepest childhood, now in a peripatetic adulthood that lives across several countries where she works a variety of menial and exhausting jobs by night in order to spend her daytimes immersed in books –

Kerninon reveals the writer's calling to be a rich and precarious one.

Surely writing is a uniquely doubt-inspiring professional endeavor. If you sell books, you're a bookseller. If you unblock drains, you're a plumber. If you practice law, you're a lawyer. How do you give yourself permission to call yourself a writer, even after writing your whole life, even after giving up material comforts in order to do it? How do you know when you've arrived, when your excessive scribbling has become a *respectable occupation*?

Once you've published your work, the questions come from outside as well. How did you become a writer? What's your daily routine? How do you write? There is always someone at a reading who wants to know the nitty-gritty of it – perhaps they, too, nourish dreams of writing and would like to know how to make their dreams a daily occupation; or perhaps they find something fishy about people being able to support themselves by making up stories. *Why you?* they seem to be asking. And indeed Kerninon has said that this book emerged from the conversations she had with readers when she published her first novel, *Buvard*, at the age of twenty-seven.

> I had no ambition except to read books and to write my own, to possess a wooden table that I could work at in the peaceful morning light, to have enough money to feed my children, enough time to love whomever I would love, and to have absolutely no one making decisions in my stead.

What could more succinctly, more lovingly, describe the life so many of us dream of? But Kerninon shows that this kind of writerly peace has to be earned in the grit of sometimes menial, non-writing-related jobs that make the dream life possible. 'There was meaning in physical work, in pain – in humiliation, even – if the payoff was freedom.'

Writing is work; work is work; reading can be work, too, for those of us who earn our livings partly by writing criticism, which can deaden the joy of it. But reading Kerninon's book has restored to me my own love of reading and its connection to my writing practice, which, it must be said, has flickered and wavered in recent years as I've stepped back from full-time bibliophilia to have my son. She writes: 'I spend my life reading books to put things back into place, to unfold myself; it's like softly singing into my own ear to wake myself up.' And stepping into Kerninon's book has helped me put my own writing life back into place, helped me unfold myself on the page, sing softly into my own ear, *it's time to get to work, it's time to get to work.*

– Lauren Elkin

A Respectable Occupation

'Personality is the repertoire of strategies that each individual develops in an effort to survive childhood.'
– Frank Sulloway, *Born to Rebel*

At the age of five and a half, I struck a deal with my father. In the first of a long and lucrative series of contracts, I agreed to stop sucking my thumb in exchange for a return trip to the capital. And yet it was my mother who took me – in my memory anyway, it was just the two of us there when she stopped suddenly in front of a building not far from Notre-Dame and made me read out the sign of *Shakespeare and Company*. That was the year we both wore fake leopard fur coats, my mother's was beautiful and heavy, with a garnet satin lining in which she would often enfold me, making a tepee for me in the cold wind, and mine was an identical soft little coat with ears on its hood and, when my mother wrapped me up in her coat, folding its two sides around me, I felt like a baby animal coming to nestle between an elder's legs, the scattered spots on our two pelts melded together, I was her little leopard girl, holding hands with my mother – all Hollywood style, glamour red, sturdy shoulders, walking like a queen – the two of us entered the shop together in step that day, and of course I remember everything. I had always vaguely known this place existed, its presence had floated somewhere in the river of my mother's words, it was the place we came from, the place we *belonged* to, that was the English verb she always used to describe the places that mattered, when she spoke she navigated by sight between the two languages, looking for the one that offered the most precise word for her emotion, inventing step by step a singsong Volapük that was my real mother tongue. *Shakespeare and Company*, she used to tell me about it all the time, we had a framed sketch of the façade hanging in the living room of our house, just like an ancestor's portrait, in fact *just next to* our ancestors' portraits – the lovely round face of her grandmother, a great-uncle who had died as a child and I knew nothing about, and then this drawing of a distant bookshop, like a family property we might have owned, our own little acre, an estate, and so when

I first set foot in it that day, I felt relieved to be able to trail my hand along the shelves and assure myself at last that they were real. In five and a half years of childhood, this was the strongest sensation I had ever felt – I had found my way back to the vessel that had brought me into the world, and when my mother lifted me up over her head to show me how there were thin mattresses on the highest and widest shelves, where lost travelling Americans could come and sleep if they needed to, everything seemed perfect to me. It was obvious you should be able to sleep among the books, that there would be no border between daily life and their pages, at home my duvet cover also had pictures of books on it, tiny little books lined up on dozens and dozens of shelves, their spines no wider than a centimetre – and so of course, of course you could sleep there, in a bookshop. There was also a wishing well, it was just perfect, my mother and I loved making wishes and lighting candles in empty chapels, throwing stones over our shoulders and simply believing in luck, and we threw some small coins into the middle of the hole dug in the ground and of course I wished I could live there, I loved everything, the smell of cigarettes like wet sand and the sliding wooden ladders, the accented modulations and intellectual snobbery of the cosmopolitan salesgirls, the little sitting room upstairs with its velvet armchairs, yes, everything really was just perfect, I was already starting to make plans in my head, I was settling in, I was just about to take off my shoes and simply take possession of my long-lost home – but then, as if she could read my mind, my mother said, all in one breath, *it's wonderful, isn't it, but we can't*. Oh I felt like I was going to fall to pieces on the spot. I clenched my fists inside my furry sleeves. Standing next to me, my mother raised her eyes to the books, lips parted, dazed, happy, like you sometimes see tourists gazing at the masterpieces in museums. It was her way of settling into contemplation, as if she could build a bench in her head and sit down on it and make herself comfortable, anywhere and anytime. And since I was her little girl, her very serious *copycat*, her miniature assistant and pupil, I also contemplated the jam-packed walls of *Shakespeare and Company*, which was not, as she would later explain, the real bookshop founded by Sylvia Beach – who was our heroine, since she had published Monsieur James Joyce – but another one, a new one, moved over from a few streets away a few years later and renamed in honour of the first one. I felt so happy that day, standing hand in hand with my mother in that place in the world that was ours, even if we couldn't stay there, because to have the right to stay there you had to be *young* and *American* and *living abroad*, three extremely abstract concepts for me at the time, and also, Mum said, because we couldn't abandon my father. Because he would die of sadness and starvation without us, and I knew this to be true. So we went back to find him – on the banks of Île Saint-Louis, a big leopard and a little leopard, delighted, confident, with all the books yet to read.

I've been living the same day for twenty-five years and I'm already thirty. When I was very small, early in the mornings, in my silky pyjamas, I would follow my father as he held my hand in the darkness of the stairway leading down to our kitchen, I let him lift me up and set me down on my chair facing him, I ate my breakfast to the babble of his radio, with my eyes fixed on a book that would have to be snatched from me without warning later so I could be taken to wash. In the shower, through the streaming water, I would seek out all the printed words, read the shampoo labels, the six sides of my mother's tampon boxes, the soft labels in my clothes. I didn't make a sound, back then, and I never really listened to anyone longer than the few seconds it took to discover a fragment of text at close range that I could read. My mother would snap her fingers to call me back to her, pulling me away from words in the same way that she pulled me out of the soapy water to stand me up in front of her and get me dressed, to button up each of the tiny snaps on the cotton *twin-sets* I insisted on wearing in winter, or to tie up the straps of the gaudy floral dresses which she hated but which I would howl blue murder to get during our fraught springtime shopping stints. As she almost forced my clothes on, my mother shook her head despairingly, but I could still see her smile – because I wasn't anybody's child, I was hers, I was my mother's tiny little girl, and she herself, when sitting for a couple of minutes in restaurant toilets unadorned with any posters, would rummage in her pockets for a banknote and systematically read both sides. That's how she was, how she is. When they were young, she and my father had hitchhiked from Cancun to Vancouver, each of them carrying a bag weighing twenty or twenty-five kilos, in which, so as not to make them even heavier, there were no books. They had been on the road for eight long months, in the sun, in rain and snow, overcoming exhaustion, food poisoning, lack of toothpaste, dew-soaked sleeping bags, stopping here or there to pick apples or cook mass-produced breakfasts in youth hostels so they could earn just enough to keep going straight ahead, just the two of them, sometimes clasped together shaking while nosy brown bears circled their tent attracted by the smell of a carton of milk, sometimes waking up in the middle of a roundabout to the face of a disgruntled sheriff, and always so happy together. But they missed books, so much so that it was painful, they were *starved* of books, my mother tells me, and she would apparently dream about throwing everything in her *backpack* away so she could fill it with novels – but in reality, they were already so laden down with the weight of their bags, they didn't have much money, they couldn't afford to buy books, so it was just hopeless. One afternoon, when her whole mind was sharpened by the absence of literature and they had been walking for hours along a road in Nebraska, my mother spied a rectangular object in the ditch and, moving with the intuition of a drug addict in withdrawal, she crawled on her stomach through the frosty grass to get hold of what was, indeed, a book.

I have heard this story a thousand times or more, and yet I don't think I ever found out which book it actually was, only that it was a book and that it was *providential*. Since my mother was better at reading in English than my father, they decided that she should start the book and read it until she reached halfway, then she would tear the book vertically down the centre of its spine to give him the first part while she read to the end, so they could talk about it together afterwards. At least that was the family legend – and this legendary quality of my family which refuses to be one is probably what I like best about it, a family of three then four, who always appear to be perfect strangers in photographs, of different nationalities even, forced to pose together in the little garden at the back of our house. In these photographs, taken by my paternal grandmother until she died and in which she always refused to be included, as if leaving the least trace of herself on earth was somehow indecent, you can see first my mother, grey-blue eyes under her blonde fringe, her face like a bird's, more pointed than the others – my father is dark, sombre, with oriental features, he never smiles at the camera, thus, no doubt in spite of himself, revealing everything that connected him to his mother. Sitting in front of them on an Adirondack chair, my little sister looks like a Swedish girl who got lost there somehow, although on a few rare snapshots her expression betrays her too, fleetingly revealing the features of an ancestor – and I'm the one leaning on the teak table, the young Mayan Indian recently adopted by Westerners, tanned, awkward. Arranged there among the flowers, our four mismatched faces show no family likeness or connection – but after all, photography and love are two distinct arts, and in spite of our incompatible faces we were happy all those years we lived together in that strange house nestled at the bottom of a provincial cul-de-sac, chosen by my mother on a whim, simply because there was a peach tree in the garden.

When I was born, my parents owned nothing, because all they had done for ten years was to save money to go to Canada, come back, save some more, and set off again pronto. They rented flats for a school year or two, lived with a mattress and two trestles, and counted the days until their next trip. When I asked my mother what they did in between times, how they spent their days, she answered that they were in love, they read books and played pinball in cafés. After my birth, between two moves, they housesat for friends who were away for a few weeks, and it was when she was exploring the neighbourhood while I was having a nap that my mother found the house, with its crudely painted 'For Sale' sign. The house had no front door, so she walked in. Inside, the place was a ruin, it was a house that no one had ever loved, where no one had ever been happy, but she went into the garden and saw the peach tree in blossom, luxurious, full of promises, standing tall among the concrete blocks like a good omen. My mother loves fruit trees, which remind her of her father's garden, with its pear boughs to which he would attach bottles so the fruit would grow inside them and he could later fill them with eau-de-vie and give them to his friends. They are all dead now. But she was probably thinking of him that day, as she had another look at the house and the scale of the damage. She didn't know it yet, but four years later she would be right there with her father, on her knees laying tiles, three weeks after delivering my sister, and when she asked him, simply to make conversation, which of his sons he felt closest to, my grandfather answered into his moustache, without looking at her: *To you*.

My mother stayed in the silent garden for a while, then went to get my father so he could also come and have a look at the tree and all the rest, and they decided to make an offer, with no hope of it ever being accepted, but maybe just as a first small step in the direction of a life to come that they knew nothing about except they now had a baby and it was probably a good idea to get a few things sorted. To their great surprise, their offer was accepted, the house was theirs, and my father went off to see my grandmother to borrow enough money to pay the notary. I imagine him running down the lane where I would later spend so much time playing with ants, and where, when I was a teenager, a young stranger tried to kill me by kneeing me in the face late one afternoon – before all that, and far more important, eternal, there is my thirty-three-year-old father running like a madman to buy the house. A few months later, the day we moved in, heavy snowflakes were falling, and with sure hands, with their broken fingernails, with those two hands that would build a whole world for us all in the years to come, my mother put in a front door to protect us, and for the first time, we had a place of our own.

The way I remember my parents best, the way I came to understand them, to grasp them in all their clarity, was perhaps during our first years together in that house, when there were still only three of us so we were not yet really a family, and when, after pancakes and brushing my hair, my father tied up my shoelaces and took me to school, before going to another school himself and joining my mother in performing tasks that were completely unknown to me, and, in the evening, the three of us would all meet back home again and read, and I wrote a bit as well, in tiny notebooks that well-intentioned people gave me as presents. Life was very simple and very beautiful, the world was populated by a man, a woman, and me, and we all lived in peace. There were lots of books and maple syrup and people called me by my name. It's only when the birth of my sister was mentioned more and more regularly that I discovered the expression *the children*, which I found very confusing, since up until then I hadn't quite understood that I was not just like them, for we all did exactly the same things – go to school and come home to read. We did everything together, used the same tools – spoons, shovels, binoculars – only mine were a bit smaller, but I had been told that I would grow, so I hadn't worried about it for a while, and in any case this information was too strange for me to really take in. I felt like we were the three bears in the Goldilocks story, bowls, chairs, beds, I loved orderly logical things, because I was the firstborn, a conservative, I liked the idea that everybody ended up finding their exact place in the world, and so to discover at six years old that I was simply still a child was not very gratifying. But I had an incredibly heavy electric typewriter my mother had lent me, and she had glued little labels with lowercase letters onto the keys because I found capitals confusing, and I wrote lots of stories about talking animals with my friend Pete. I wrote minimal poems and letters to people I liked. My room in the attic, painted a translucent green, was full of books and bits of paper – the books were those my mother had stacked up in there, the summer before I started primary school, and I remember how we looked at each other one day when we were standing together gazing at that monument of pages that she had piled up in my room. At that moment, there was something in her eyes that was pleading but annoyed at itself for pleading, something that didn't want to impose anything on such a little girl but was afraid it might not want anything more to do with her if she didn't rise to the challenge. It was the first time I saw my mother being simply herself, being so vulnerable that I engraved her in my memory, blonde, pregnant with my sister, stunning, standing in front of the loot she had assembled to tell me who she really was. An identical monument of books had saved her as well, thirty years earlier, from a hopeless childhood, and so she spread her secret before me, she explained what she loved most in the world, in a gesture that was also a potlatch, an immeasurably generous offering, which I might be expected to return one day with an even greater gift.

I imagine I smiled, but I don't know. All I know is that as soon as I learned the alphabet I read her books, I explored every corner of the palace she had built for me, I lost myself there and found myself again, I did everything in my power to satisfy her, to repair her, to recompense her for the enormous effort it must have cost her to make all this known to her first child. I read. I read books non-stop, in a panicked frenzy, trying to catch up on lost time, trying to catch up with my mother who seemed to know everything. A few months later, after slamming the door to my bedroom, where she had shut me in to punish me for cutting the fabric of the sofa with my pinking shears – with my friend Joseph, this time, as an innocent attempt to be simply childish, aged seven, perhaps – she immediately opened it again to add that I was not allowed to read during my punishment, for at the time we both knew full well that being shut in a room for two hours was the one thing I loved most in the world, the thing I did all the time of my own free will, because being alone in a room was the ideal situation for reading. The three of us did just this every weekend in the silent house, my father lying on his big wooden bed on the ground floor, with a massive historical tome and a bar of chocolate, my mother curled up on the mezzanine, deep in her current book which could be absolutely anything at all, she read everything, she had no memory for anything else, not even, later on, for the years my sister and I were born. She had studied very little, officially, but her knowledge of books was colossal, dazzling. In a way, I think I've never met anyone who knows as much on the subject, anyone whose understanding of literature is as direct, physical, instinctive. As I write these words, I've spent ten years more than she has in tertiary education, and we diverge on a number of other points, but then as now, her mastery of grammar, her intuitive knowledge of English and French linguistics, and the pertinence of her comments seem infallible to me. Born in a little fishing village, the oldest and only girl in a family of four children, she learned Russian at boarding school when she was ten and read everything she could, every day, every night. My mother is my thesaurus, even now. When I gave her my first pieces of writing to read as a teenager, she could precisely cite which lines I had plagiarised from my favourite author of the moment. In any given paragraph, she would always point her finger at the right place – the place where I had been lazy. When one of my experimental exercises consisted in writing a piece deliberately packed with adjectives and adverbs to create a *cloying, saturated* effect, as I claimed, she said that it was *no use* justifying myself to her and explaining that I had done it on purpose – she said that, if one day someone was stupid enough to *intentionally* make up an orchestra with only drum sets, even if they said they had wanted it to be that way, the sound would still not be worth listening to. I wrote another book in which she thought there were too many characters, and then another where there weren't enough, one where nothing happened, and another where impossible things happened, for she was willing to admit that sometimes things happen in life that you couldn't make into a believable story, even if this fact clashed with something deep inside her, but all the same, she was implacable, she would not change her mind. If I lost a manuscript and went crazy with panic, she would just shrug with no compassion at all and explain that in any case I would have to throw away or lose lots of books before writing a single good one. *The best thing that can happen to you is a house fire.* It was she who convinced me to give up on describing my characters physically, arguing that in the perfect horror novels she had read, the monstrous creatures are only described through the noises they make, or the smell they give off, or even the texture of their skin or their temperature, and in that silence, readers best devise the intimate monsters that really frighten them personally, because no one can exactly imagine what frightens anyone else.

There was a second lesson inside the first one. Behind my mother's belief that it was important to leave the reader some space in a book, there was the vague but persistent idea that other people were in fact impenetrable, that there should be some means to understand them and to be understood by them, but that these means were even more complex than the problem they were supposed to solve, and that it was therefore safer to stay away from any activity that included other human beings – with the notable exception of love. People were vague, unreliable, and more devious than us. Discernible behind each of their transparent sentences were others, and those were apparently the ones we should have heard, but we could never understand why and so we refused to do so, that was our luxury, we were very, very lucky, she told me, because we had books and, in books, the sentences were eternal, black on white, solid, credible – they weren't *up in the air*, they didn't come out of nowhere, they had been polished, ordered, thought through by precise, attentive individuals, and they offered up the whole world, the accelerated, perfected world, washed clean of its dross, with no downtime, a pure and bouncing stream, a world into which we could escape whenever the real world stopped being interesting, which happened all too often when someone came to talk to us. And that lesson was a great lesson too, for someone who wanted to become a writer. It was reinforced, in fact almost illustrated, by my father's panicked but reasonably well hidden fear of the outside world – it wasn't so long ago that, standing behind him in a patisserie at Christmastime, I saw his ears blush slightly when he was placing his order, because communicating causes him, as it does me, minuscule and permanent problems – but then you would have to go back even further and recount how my frightened, starched paternal grandmother would trot through the aisles of department stores as fast as she could to escape the affable salesgirls, happy as she was to talk only to us every week, or how she soaked her opaque stockings in the Atlantic ocean one day during a heatwave because, at the age of seventy-nine, she was still afraid of being judged for her lack of morality and indecency by the whole beach if anyone noticed that she had taken them off during the day. My imperious grandmother, with her face like a humiliated Native American, which gradually became my own face. My grandmother, who was somehow purified in her later years, suddenly liberated of all her worries. I can still see her sitting obediently in an armchair in the retirement home she had to be moved to in the end – after she had been found wandering in the train station of our town, bloodied, her coat pockets full of banknotes and strange little objects tied up in elastic bands, a caught fugitive, captured by those who loved her – sitting in her armchair and looking at us attentively, my little sister Maria and me, as we gave her a sparkly manicure, barely five months before she died – this woman whose severity was so elegant, this timid and unhappy person who is my direct ancestor and about whom I was thinking continuously the first year I lived alone, my first year as a writer, completely isolated, miles away from what had always been my home, renting a huge and almost empty apartment looking out over one of the main thoroughfares of Budapest, the dwelling where I lovingly repeated my grandmother's daily routine, where I trained myself tirelessly to be as diligent, as solitary, as full of the same stony pride.

We were in the bedroom of a rental holiday house one day when my mother said to me: *You say you want to be a writer, but it's been a long time since I've heard the sound of your typewriter. You need to get to work, because that's what writers do, they work, you know*, and I was so mortified I started getting up at half five to have enough time to read before leaving for school, and I would write for several hours every evening before going to bed, eating apples all the while. I ate tons of apples, and the cores piled up on my desk in a solid thing that my mother once took for a wooden sculpture. She would come in and flit around me like an agitated hummingbird, darting her wide-open eyes at the apple cores, but in fact she was probably just curious about what was going on, irresistibly attracted by the long-desired sound of the keys, and I stayed riveted to my machine, just as when I was a little girl I had stayed stretched out on my bed in my room with a book lightly resting on my belly button, feeling so much in the right place, so complete.

I soon started reading constantly, reading everywhere, all the time, even if it was noisy or dark, in an organised, excessive, impatient way, jumping from one book to the next like they were lily pads, studying by myself, conducting an inquiry. It was during that period that I regularly went out in the evenings to recite poetry in cafés, and that was yet another apprenticeship, standing there on a stage, rather than sitting at a desk, and holding a whole text by heart in my memory as if I were leading a flock of sheep with the help of sheepdogs, saying it in public, composing music with the sentences. And, maybe because I was really young at the time, the old poets who were the heart of that notorious club took me under their wing. Legend had it that they had all met at Narcotics Anonymous – which probably just means somewhere near Pigalle – and they educated me, transformed me, constructed me. What I owe them, how much I loved them, I could never truly say, even though I see them only rarely now, for far too many reasons. Their first meeting place was an old biscuit factory in my hometown, and that's why I've sometimes thought of myself as an industrial process, a mysterious machine, with my masters carefully setting the rollers, tightening nuts and bolts, adding elements, oiling my cogs, testing prototypes, but managing little by little to collect and assemble the different pieces that would compose me in the end. It was a second education – after my house full of books, the world. I regularly took the train to go and see them in Paris, I was sixteen and a half, one or another of them would meet me on the platform at Montparnasse station, settle me into a taxi or a van or an old hearse they had picked up for a song, and we would criss-cross the capital while reading poems to each other. They exchanged me like a ransom at each stop, I would go from apartment to rooftop, from rooftop to pavement café, we didn't sleep, we walked for hours, I tagged along with them to buy heroin when they needed a fix and they put their hands over my eyes because they didn't want me to see, they taught me how to walk in high heels like a woman, how to recite texts with a matchstick in my mouth in order to improve my diction, how to open oysters, we would go to museums as well, or sometimes to the butcher to buy offal for a gory performance piece, and I would go back to school, exhausted by the sleepless nights, and feeling frantic, dazzled, impatient.

I turned seventeen, eighteen, nineteen, twenty. We were only meeting infrequently when, a few weeks before the publication of my first book under a pseudonym, I celebrated the event in Paris with two of them and a third from the same circle – whom I only knew by sight and reputation, a poet-performer with astounding energy, exiled from Southeast Asia – to whom the other two started telling the story of how they had literally found me in that factory transformed into a cultural space, at a time when my eye make-up made me look like a racoon and I had never heard anyone play Chopin. The one whose place we were at that night was a pianist, and once, when I was still very young and he lived in the rue Marie-et-Louise, in a studio whose principal drawback was that the shower was almost in the middle of the room and so, in order to avoid the temptation of looking, and so I could get undressed without fearing his adult eyes, he had sat himself down at his piano to play with his back to me while I was lathering myself with soap.

That was the kind of thing they talked about that night – what we were like at the time, and all the adventures we'd had together. They talked about it all, and I remembered everything and felt rich and blessed to have had so many good times, to have been tolerated in spite of all logic, and yet when the pianist proudly declared that, even as a twelve-year-old, I was already writing at the same frantic pace as now – which was not true, of course, but what is a poet, after all, if not someone who exaggerates for the beauty of the gesture? – the third one gave me a look full of pity. *Why would anyone write at twelve years old?* he asked without looking at me. *When I was twelve, if you want to know, I was screwing girls in the mountains. Because that's the only sensible thing to do at twelve. Not writing.* And then, in the middle of my triumph, in a single instant, I felt miserable, frenetic, absurd, but there was nothing more to say, so we stayed almost silent until it was time to leave for the party given by my publisher that evening, and there, in the tight Parisian crowd, an empty plastic cup in hand, that poet whom I had known for all of four hours, and whose writing relentlessly described his flight on foot from Cambodia to Paris – although I'm still not sure whether that was actually what happened or under those conditions – that poet looked straight at me silently for a moment and then, just before leaving without saying goodbye to anyone, briefly placed his lips on mine, which was another diploma in its own way.

After that, I stopped wondering what would happen to me. I decided to take everything as it comes. I continued to read in the mornings and write at night. Gertrude Stein had declared: 'If you don't work hard when you are twenty, no one will love you when you are thirty,' and because I thought that was true, when I was twenty I came and confronted my father, one evening, in the kitchen where he used to pour milk so serenely into my cereal bowl and, looking him straight in the eye, I negotiated a *gap year*, I demanded a break from university, because I was young and full of life and I wanted to know if I could really be a writer, if I was capable of doing that, seriously, as a job, as a priority, as a responsibility, daily. To my great surprise, my father laid down his weapons very quickly and simply asked: *Go where?*

Like many children, I had classified my father, from the very start and on principle, in the category of certainties. Not only was he the first person I ever saw in my life – my mother being drugged up from the caesarean – but chance and fate gave me a particularly predictable father, although strangely not to himself, which tends to make him rather anxious. Very early on, I could have created a Joseph Cornell box to represent him: his favourite colours (black, maroon and blue-green set side by side), his favourite textures (roughness of denim, corduroy, my mother's skin), his beverages (Guinness, tea with milk), his weaknesses (chocolate, beurre blanc with shallots, green onions), his music (bass guitar or trumpet), his noises (whistling, rubbing unshaven cheeks, heavy tread through the rooms of our house), his smells (rain on tarmac or gravel roads, leather and earth from Habit Rouge by Guerlain). For a long time, my father was a perfectly defined territory for me, in which I felt I could move with the same flexibility as when I was a child and used to climb up his body like a kitten. In the mornings, he would methodically pile up his bread rolls in front of himself before buttering them; when he needed to take a plane, he would go to the airport exactly two hours before the recommended time, and then as now he knew all the social security numbers of the whole family off by heart. The paternal laws were as strange taken separately as they were consistent taken together, yet children are not insensitive to the pleasures of repetition and so for years we understood each other perfectly. Just recently, after accidentally stepping barefoot on a rusty nail, I disinfected the wound and then went to find my health record booklet to check that my tetanus immunisation was up to date, and I wondered whether I would ever stop being the very obedient daughter of my very cautious father. Probably not. There is something slightly autistic in all this, which often makes us look ridiculous from the outside, but in fact my father taught me how to write books without him even realising it – with his infinite caution, his timidity, his way of thinking through all the possible options before taking the smallest decision – without knowing it, he filled my quiver with the precise arrows that I would come to need later on.

The day I left for Budapest, in 2007, for an eighteen-hour bus trip, in the early hours of the morning, he said goodbye to me in the parking lot and we were both crying with dry eyes. While he was loading my baggage, he was afraid, as I was, but neither of us was capable of saying so, and we both knew that I would not be coming back, that this was the end of the life we had shared.

That year, I understood something else about my family: I became aware of our stone-hard atavism, our limited view of things, our fierce intolerance, but also how only that intractability could open up a clear horizon for me, once and for all. In Budapest, I shut myself in, I would only go out to stretch my legs on the main streets in the frozen snow, and I thought lovingly about my grandmother forever walking in circles in her favourite park, feeding the ducks and the swans at regular hours, a long way away. But in fact, I didn't miss anyone and I wrote two books. It was a very good year because I was twenty years old and it was the first time I could just read and write all day for months, with no interruptions, no classes to attend, no invitations, no phone calls. I thought that to be a writer, I had to train like an athlete, like a dancer, until it didn't hurt any more, until I didn't ask myself any more questions. I wanted to possess that skill. I had already studied literature at university for three years to satisfy paternal demands, I had submitted, passed, proved myself, but what was the point, since in fact I had no ambition except to read books and to write my own, to possess a wooden table that I could work at in the peaceful morning light, to have enough money to feed my children, enough time to love whomever I would love, and to have absolutely no one making any decisions in my stead. In Budapest, I had an enormous empty apartment in Rákóczi út and a table in front of a window where I sat all day writing. I was alone in the world. I had no schedule. I woke up and sat down at my desk, I worked until lunchtime, I started again, and then almost every other day I would take the metro to the Institut Français on the other side of the river to borrow books. I read all the books I hadn't had the time to read when I was busier, I read books about painting, Hungary, biographies, novels, I bought cigarettes and went home to write all night. One sunny January morning, I celebrated my twenty-first birthday all alone in that city where I knew no one, and now I always think about that year when I'm trying to reassemble myself, to remember who I am. When I'm afraid of being alone, when I'm not sure I can finish a piece of writing, when I feel I'm in danger, I always come back to the young woman I was in Budapest, ten years ago, working away without worrying about anything except books to read and write, the woman no one except me can even remotely remember.

I went back to live in Budapest, five years ago, in a new apartment on the other side of the river this time, in Buda, on the sixth and top floor of a yellow building in Attila street. I spent six months there reading, going swimming in the open-air pool of the Császár-Komjádi sports centre, eating tinned beans in paprika sauce, and babysitting the two little girls of a super-wealthy businesswoman in the cosmetics industry whose apartment dominated the city from the top of an elegant hill which I ascended at the end of the day in a kind of cable car blindly making its way through the verdant boughs of trees, and later in the evening, my hands covered in pastry dough or ink stains from felt pens, I would go home in a taxi and put the last words, the most important words, to the novel I had written the first draft of during the year I had spent in the city and whose publication two years later would change everything for me. I wrote almost a chapter a day, never had writing seemed so obvious, so easy, as if I were suddenly being rewarded after years of writing, I was continually learning new things, how to write dialogue, how to create endings, plot twists, it was incredible, my life was minimalistic, it fit into a suitcase, and I was very happy. Two months after I turned twenty-five, a good thirty centimetres of snow fell, and miles away, my paternal grandmother died in her sleep, and barely a few days later, scandalously, indecently, I decided to fall in love. It was in that state that I wrote all night, sitting cross-legged in a wide beige armchair stuck in a corner by the window. I really loved writing in that spot – I spent a lot of time there and finished a novel – but I also remember having written good work, long ago, glued to a radiator for a whole winter in the Black Country in England, in a freezing Georgian house whose age made it impossible to fix the failing insulation, and on whose front steps the local street whores would always sit to gossip *between two shifts*, as my Albanian flatmate Odeta would say, the one who also gave me this poignant and mysterious saying, which I have never forgotten: *No one gives back the freedom you've given away to them.* We all called her Ode, I liked her a lot, she was brilliant and hard and wrote extraordinary jolting poems, while another poet, Helen, also wrote in another room and would later publish a sparkling collection, and while her boyfriend at the time painted continuously in a little room facing the garden, wearing all of his clothes on top of each other, covered by a poncho to fight off the terrible cold of the Midlands in February. I wrote a book in bed that winter, leaning back against the radiator in my room, just as I later wrote on a sofa bathed in sunlight in Rome, where, together with a girl I hardly knew, I decided to give up on men for Italian wine and also, before that, in a little café with a veranda on the banks of the Landwehrkanal in Berlin, when I was living at number 7 Maybachufer, a stormy year, when my flatmate Alcacer was an ex-lover and apprentice-director with whom I had rows every day, but under the glass roof of the Café Condé that now no longer exists, just like the Berlin I knew, I sometimes wrote good pages, and also at night, when I took speed for four days straight to edit a whole manuscript and Alcacer would come and knock on my door every morning when he woke up to tell me *what day it is today*, and even in the ruined one-bedroom apartment I rented the following year in Nantes, when an enormous part of my life had fallen apart, to the point that I accepted returning to where I had started out.

When I got there, distressed, dishonoured, I started tutoring a restless sixteen-year-old boy, I didn't know exactly what I was supposed to do with him, until his mother called and said: *The most important thing, really, is that you calm him down*. And so, for six months, I was a teacher of calm – me, the anxious, the excessive, the turbulent one. I tried to teach him the only calm I knew, which was that of the printed word. I read John Fante aloud to him, Hemingway, Fitzgerald, Steinbeck, Bernhard, Dickinson and experimental poetry. It wasn't enough to make ends meet, so I took a second job in a restaurant, in the evenings. After work – which, besides carrying plates, consisted mainly in cutting up gherkins to the sound of the chef yelling – I would go dancing in scummy nightclubs, get home very late, very tired, very alone, and painstakingly find my way through the sum total of my worldly possessions strewn all over the floor, because at that time, I thought I was too busy picking myself up to pick anything else up, because I loved without hope, because I didn't know what to do any more, I was a very confused and unhappy young woman, when I went home to do my laundry and drink tea my father would ask me: *What is to become of you?* And I silently thought, *I don't know.* I was twenty-three years old, no one loved me, no one thought I would write any more books, and I declared everything was fine, got into my sofa-bed with my shoes on and a can of Red Bull, and rewrote a novel into the early morning.

It really is the same day every day, only the places change, to the point where when I look out the window, I am hardly capable of knowing exactly where I am. Five years ago, in Budapest, I finished my novel, and I came to live in Paris, where after a very short time I found myself violently punching the guy I thought I loved and who was the only reason I had come to that city, which is a strange thing in itself and I'm still not sure whether I should regret it or not. I only remember shouting at him that I hadn't left the west bank of the Danube, the east bank of the Spree, the perfect hills of Devon or the lanterns of Monte Testaccio to be insulted. After his precipitous departure, in my little room with no hot water and a ceiling light decorated with a sketch of a phallus, I wrote a poem affirming that women, like cockroaches, can survive anything, and it was true, more or less. I worked multiple jobs, ate lots of dehydrated Chinese noodles, and three months later, I was busy emptying that room to move into a tiny studio apartment, but one with a balcony, when a voice from a telephone announced that my book was accepted.

Typing, my daily activity for twenty-five years, is a discipline that I never really acquired. My mother could do it perfectly, she once read a whole handbook about it – I could joke that she read it simply because it was the only book she could lay her hands on that day, but that would reduce her to an anecdote without really understanding her – because she is the kind of person who scrupulously learns how to do something, who reaches full mastery and then stops, and can only do it well from that moment onwards. She tried to teach me, obviously, and I sometimes seek to forgive myself by saying that, at six years old, I might have been a bit too young to learn something like that, that my hands were simply too small for me to succeed, but in fact I know that it was because I was already me: someone much too impetuous to devote herself to precision. Throughout my whole life I feel like I never really learned anything, I only ever did things halfway unless they appeared essential to me, my handwriting is illegible despite my father's shouts still ringing in my ears, because I was his first born, because the burden of everything rested upon me, I was the measure of his survival, the gold standard of his success. I drive without ever looking in the rear-view mirrors, I don't understand irony, I don't perceive facial microexpressions, I am not subtle, ever, I speak the same English now as I spoke when I was ten, a language full of profanities and approximations with which I can always get by, in three different accents depending on the circumstances, each of them honourable, accents were never a problem in any language, but there's no margin for me to make any progress, I've always loved the same things, I don't know how to change, I'm like a stone under water, the most I can hope for is to become *rounder* as I get worn down, but the one and only thing that interests me in any activity is to go fast. I've seen my mother be capable of everything: sawing wood with precision, sanding, varnishing, nailing it, cutting and laying tiles, making roasts with pastry crusts in rental kitchens or mobile homes, skydiving, swallowing fire, driving on the left, finding her way anywhere, standing up to men – in the kitchen of our family home, which was recently sold to strangers, there is a ceramic tile that was cracked by the cast iron teapot she once threw across the room to frighten my father who, I think, was shouting too loud and too long that day – but I never understood, I never really understood that she had succeeded in all these things by first failing. I was a little girl, she was an adult woman and a mother leopard – our ambitions and our needs were very different. If she had dealt with things as vehemently and impatiently as I did, our house would have been a shipwreck. But because she was already in her thirties when we could start talking and getting acquainted, all my mother's years of apprenticeship had escaped me. I never saw her learning, I never knew anything of her repeated failures – all I have ever known of my mother is her infallibility and the grace with which she deploys it and which, luckily or unluckily, conveyed the certainty that I as her child also possessed it, naturally, when I don't even have a feature of her face and was not even recognised as her offspring at customs at Chicago airport, in the spring of 1997, during a night in transit on our way to Canada. The suspicious officials couldn't believe that we belonged together, since we didn't have the same surname and nothing in our faces made us look as if we were of the same family – my mother's high Slavic cheekbones and seashell complexion, and my dark hair, southern complexion and slanted smiling eyes – nothing in our faces could convince them of our being related except our floods of tears when faced with their incredulity. My mother rose to that challenge too, once again I saw her win the day, in the end, and take me with her. On that day I was already exactly the same person as I am today, I typed just as fast and just as badly, I only thought about books, and I started adopting the British Columbian accent as soon as we landed. From Chicago she took me to Vancouver as if it were a pilgrimage, so that at age ten I too could contemplate the orange building in the morning light, which was the first thing she had seen on landing in that city with my father almost twenty years previously. She always talked about it as an event, that building, as an instant when she felt her life belonged to her at last, and it was an event for me as well when I saw it, an epiphany.

Like *Shakespeare and Company*, British Columbia is another of my family's imaginary provinces. It's the place in the world where my parents lived the longest *of their own free will*, and the reason we all speak English. With each other, sometimes, but mostly to ourselves. We each have our own English. My father first learned his through music, then at university in Brest, and finally on the roads separating Canada from Mexico. The tone of his voice remains the same, his grammar is impeccable but his accent is the most recognisable of all of ours. My mother, for her part, learned English in high school, from her travels, and especially from books. Her accent is good, but she speaks a bit too slowly, and the timbre of her voice betrays her. She makes *absolutely* no grammar mistakes, and she can describe in detail the whys and wherefores of each of the pitfalls she managed to avoid on her way. My sister learned English as a baby, then as a little girl in campsites in Cornwall, then at school in New York and San Francisco, and finally at the University of Vancouver and from *Gone With the Wind*. Between the ages of thirteen and twenty-one, she spent so much time across the Atlantic that my father used to talk about going ahead and just buying her a jet in order to save money on all the plane tickets. She has a British Columbian accent and is perfectly undetectable. She mostly eats American food she prepares herself. She once told me she had never been cross in English. She feels like the language is another dimension for her, in which she can finally be at peace.

She was just starting to learn it, however, that summer when we drove up from Poole to Inverness, the town where Shakespeare set Macbeth's murder of King Duncan, but also the place where we could eat deep-fried Mars bars, which we couldn't wait to try. We'd spent five summers criss-crossing the United Kingdom by then, in a second-hand Renault Express that my mother had outfitted so we could sit inside it to have lunch when it rained – in other words, all the time. We camped under downpours and hiked to see waterfalls my father found on his secret maps. But that was the last year we would spend together in the verdant lanes of Albion, and we knew it. In September I would be going to university, I was, in some way, on the threshold of my adult life. Something very important happened that summer – I can't remember where exactly, somewhere or other on one of our many stops on the long journey from Dorset to Scotland – maybe because of the rain that was a feature of all my childhood holidays, we entered a bookshop, and the book was there. I saw it immediately, just like my mother did twenty years earlier on that road in Nebraska. The grey-blue spine, in the fine matte paper of Faber & Faber. The author's name, in white, Ted Hughes, and the title, *Birthday Letters*, in incendiary red. Taking it off the shelf, I started out, without knowing it, on a very long journey.

The first sentence I managed to make out, in that English which I spoke but was not yet used to reading, floored me: 'At twenty-five, I was dumbfounded afresh / By my ignorance of the simplest things.' And I, who knew even less, plunged in head-first. I read the book in the car, jolting along on backroads meandering between menacing lochs, on the ferry taking us back to France, and also the following month, in the fragile house by the seaside that my paternal grandfather had unilaterally chosen and where my grandmother, after the untimely death of her husband, continued spending her summers. I was with her, reading those poems, trying to write my own as well, alone with her as we talked and made apple tarts, we were like two elderly sisters with a peaceful daily routine, and it never happened again, she was never the same afterwards. I read the book over and over, I translated passages from it, I learned some of it off by heart – because I had never, ever seen anything like it. Like signposts, books lead us to other books, they make us ricochet – we read like Dante letting Virgil guide him in the wild forest of sin. In libraries, in bookshops, seeing them all there, side by side, so clear, like niches in a columbarium, each one encasing a voice, an aria, I don't know anything better. I always return to them. That's it.

These days I always read in the morning, for hours, in bed, a technical miracle I owe to another lesson learned from a much loved man: *the main thing is to have free time – you'll obviously work out how to earn a crust somehow – but free time is something you'll always have to scavenge*, he told me earnestly. And so, aged nineteen, armed with this piece of informed advice and the new conviction that money was the key to free time, which was and would remain my greatest need, I borrowed my grandmother's car to go and work on the coast for the summer, and I remember how astounded I was by the simple fact of being on the middle of a motorway bathed in sunshine driving a car towards my place of employment, because I had never ever, never, ever, ever believed that I would grow up one day and be legally allowed to do such a thing.

I was a waitress, and I worked without knowing exactly what I was doing. I accepted the lack of sleep, the shifts, the exhaustion that prevented me from reading, I accepted the aching muscles that woke me up at night when my boyfriend came to stay and we slept in a caravan that rocked under the weight of his towering body, and then, very quickly, I fell in love with someone else, I destroyed all my former life, I served mojitos and told obscene jokes in a café on the Atlantic coast with exemplary regularity, simply so I could stay in the same place as the man I now loved. I did that for five years, how can I describe it exactly, university in the winter and, in the summers, the little house where I lived with four other girls, group dynamics, the labour of lifting cast iron tables at the end of the night and turning them upside down to stack them along the terrace, forearms varnished with the sugar from cocktails, love, insomnia, bruises, sunburn, living back to front, going to work when the sun was setting and getting up at midday to eat shellfish. Twice each summer, on payday, all the girls from the bar, in a miraculous and tacit reprieve, went to the competing watering hole and drank margaritas all afternoon. We didn't talk about anything, we drank through our straws, in a couple of hours we were all drunk and happy, and then one of us would say, *Shall we go for a swim?*, and we would take off for the beach in an orderly phalanx – young, invincible, tanned, the thrill of being five or six Valkyries in the cobbled streets, marching together towards the overcrowded beach – and there was no need for a single word, all the boundaries were smashed between our diverse and complicated personalities, the one who lacked self-confidence, the perfectionist, the way too over-sensitive one, no more bullshit, *basta*, all of us levelled by the strength of the tequila, all warriors marching straight towards the water, taking off our clothes without stopping in our tracks, five or six dresses pulled over the top of our heads in synchrony, with no comments, our teeth clenched from the alcohol, when we got to the waves we were wearing nothing but our knickers and we floated on our backs, screaming, while our regular clientele on the beach couldn't believe their eyes, this exhibitionist herd of impalas that had thrown themselves into the water, exactly like animals, with the same impenetrable bliss, the same indifference to anything that was not our own skin or not pure pleasure – swimming and then getting out, shaking ourselves dry, putting our clothes back on as impeccably as we had taken them off, tying up wet hair, and going to work in a serried rank as if nothing at all had happened. Later on, after the bar had shut, in the first hours of the morning, in the clinking of boats in the marina, I would stand in my summer dress on an empty terrace and throw small coins against a first floor hotel window to wake up the man who was sleeping there, felled by hard work, so he would come down and open the side door and I could go up with him to his bed filled with cigarettes, sweets, teaspoons, sand, where we caressed each other with our blistered hands, the tender contact of skin, to forget wiping glasses for hours, forget the steam, the lemon juice on broken skin, the dead weight of beer crates, the noise. There was an inexplicable hole in the room's parquet floor that allowed us to watch the foreign guests in the restaurant below having their breakfast of fresh bread in the mornings, while we were lying on our stomachs and doing it one last time before our shifts started, and I never felt so alive.

Fundamentally, I didn't know anything about anything, but I worked, like a dog, and at the end of the second summer, with all that money and a few gifts from scattered family members, I was able to write for practically a whole year without having to worry about anything, and I did it again the next year, and the year after that, and for five years running, I was a waitress and a writer, and always felt exactly in the right place because I was split, balanced at last, repaying my tribute to my poor ancestors. When my maternal grandfather, who was still alive then, made jokes with my uncles about my never-ending studies, I could counter-attack by telling him the details of cleaning out the rubbish bins at my café, kneeling on the rusty metal, the bleach, my hands covered in sores, I laid them down at his feet in a gesture of restoration, of respect, I came to lay my minuscule offering down at his wounded plasterer's feet, trying to find my place. I had never lived anywhere except in books before becoming a waitress by accident, I was a profoundly inept person, but in a few summers, I developed my skills, I multiplied them, I discovered my atavistic potential as a servant – I experienced sweat, and it wasn't just an experience, it was a promotion. There was meaning in physical work, in pain – in humiliation, even – if the payoff was freedom. And, most of all, there was real pleasure in being able to talk with the men in my clan on an equal footing, in no longer being seen as simply the city girl, the one with soft hands, the *bookish* one. I was one of them, at least partly, and I adored those years, I grieved for them, and I am exactly that, I am also that, the girl of five summers crushed by love and alcohol, the one who *does things*, and knows that this is the only reason I can write books.

Recently, one of the last times I went to see my maternal grandmother, I had put on a suit that I hoped would satisfy her expectations, but it was all pointless, for as soon as I got there she ordered me to go into the garden shed and get a basket because it was time to pick the apples. And so we walked together to the bottom of the garden around the house where my mother had grown up, down to the old apple tree I had climbed every summer as a child to spend the afternoons in peace and quiet, and I climbed it once again, in my suit and high heels, to pick apples and throw them into the sack she was holding out to me a few metres below. I was there in the tree, halfway up, as I always seem to feel in fact, the daughter of teachers, with my dark hair and my dark eyes, my glowing health, standing in the branches at twenty-nine years of age, always halfway between what I am and where I've come from, the vast world, the big words from university, the indecent splendour of the Danube in the morning, and those two lines of Robert Frost, 'Magnified apples appear and disappear / Stem end and blossom end,' and my grandfather, dying, disfigured, stupefied, weighing thirty-six kilos, after trying to treat what he didn't know was a tumour in his mouth with a metal file.

I don't understand anything. I've given up trying to understand. I am stupid and stubborn like an old Breton woman, probably because that's what I'm destined to become in the end. I'll finish up living in a cabin by a lake with my sister – she's promised this to me several times – living that dream life we will have, *when the men have died*, as she says in a strangely joyful voice when talking about the premature loss of our respective future husbands. I'll end up speechless, on my knees in front of a great meadow, like a peasant woman in Thomas Hardy. In the meantime, I'll write fiction as long as I am able to, but I still have itchy feet sometimes at the idea of being back there, standing in the café once again, young and intact and insomniac, for after all, it's thanks to the accumulated loot from the café that I can read, every morning, in the first hours of the day, like I did when I was a child, at twelve, at seventeen, at twenty, twenty-five, twenty-eight, always. I spend my life reading books to put things back into place, to unfold myself, it's like softly singing into my own ear to wake myself up.

I don't know what this all means, I only know that I stagger under its weight as I write it, that I wash it, hold it up to the light, that I honour it in my own way by this forlorn gesture of bearing witness to it. Putting things into words, setting past events into sentences – it's my great-grandmother's crown of orange blossom, framed in our living room, fixed, inoffensive, yet not saying anything about the reality of a failed marriage, of a husband drowning his love for another woman in alcohol, of the frozen earth, of brutal animals, of sharecropping. Stories are only stories, they allow us to catch our breath but they don't repair anything, they are what can be cobbled together with the bits of debris found after catastrophes, they are not a second chance, just the praise of the dead whispered into the ears of the survivors, as eloquent as it is forlorn. I'm making a crown of orange blossom. And leaving it behind.

Both my parents believed in books, believed in solitude, inner life, patience, luck, they believed in the power of a wooden plank solidly fixed into an alcove in my bedroom on which to put my typewriter, in fact, perhaps they even liked the *noise* of the electric machine when it rattled out, all in one go, the sentence I had just written into the tiny screen above the keys. In my family, no one had ever earned enough money to have any faith in it, so they didn't believe in money, they believed in travel, poetry, material simplicity, they believed that literature was a respectable occupation. Having come along first, because I was the oldest, I took on board what was most obvious, without yet knowing the weight of that golden choice which could never really be one, but I've been writing for far too long now to still be paying dues for my decision. I write because of the sad old man who, in a dance hall in Birmingham, took out a piece of paper from his pocket to show it to me, a very old, tatty piece of paper that he delicately unfolded in his clammy hands, and it was a letter the Irish poet Seamus Heaney had written to him when he was nineteen to tell him he had talent. He couldn't even cry any more, he had cried so much. He seemed to have exhausted his supply of tears. I write because of little Lilly in *The Hotel New Hampshire* by John Irving, when she says: 'I'm not a maid, I'm a writer.' I write because of Jo March eating her apples and reading, perched in a tree far away from her sisters. I write books because it's good discipline, because I like sentences and I like putting things in order in a Word document, I like counting the words every night, and I like finishing what I start. I write books because, whether they're mine or someone else's, they are what interests me the most. I respect Hemingway more than anyone, perhaps because he committed suicide, and because, like him, I don't know how to live, I don't know how to survive, and also perhaps because, in the words of the amiable proprietress of the house in Seine-Maritime where my partner and I hoped to get some rest one weekend, I'm bonkers. *She's slightly unbalanced, isn't she?* she asked the man I love with a big smile, as if I were no longer in the room, as if the simple fact that I was a writer took me out of the world of emotions as surely as a maître d'hôtel taking me by the arm and seeing me to the door, as if I could feel no pain. In his preface to a collection of extracts from *L'Autre Journal*, Michel Butel discusses his abnormal, literary life with a precision that made me burst into tears when I read it a few months ago. He writes: 'As a child, I didn't speak to anyone. I didn't listen to anyone. I read. I read day and night. I read newspapers. I read books. I didn't study. And so I didn't want a career. I knew nothing about those stories, careers, studies, salaries, schedules, normal life. I couldn't even see there was such a thing as a normal life. And yet, it was all around me. It was set against my abnormal life. I felt threatened. But that worrying, painful sensation didn't change anything about my abnormal life. Quite the contrary. So I persisted in reading. Books. Newspapers. Because I loved them all. In those days I loved all the books I read. I loved all the newspapers I read. In those days ... Because I could find everything there ... The explanations that no one had given me. The meaning of my name, of my ancestors' name, the meaning of the words I heard (without listening to them). The reason for the never-ending attacks I endured in the name of normal life. The so-called sixth sense that helped me to predict them and protect myself. The meaning of beauty, which I didn't know anything about, which I couldn't see anywhere around me before books taught me how to discover it, the meaning of justice, which was impossible to find until newspapers revealed it to me as persecuted, martyred. Books and newspapers talked to me at night, in the daytime. Now sometimes, miraculously, I can still hear the life of books and newspapers from my childhood. In those moments, I weep.' And I weep with Butel, who is one of the great men of my life. I didn't accept normal life either, I never believed in it. Wherever I've lived, I've moved with my load of books, it's a shifting continent of which I am the only map, and often, before settling down to work, I reread a few favourite passages to form a circle around me, I try to stand upright in its centre, to honour those I love. Books are like closed boxes to me, with terribly sibylline and exciting labels, and I am a curious sort, although perhaps exclusively in this area, I want to know what's inside them, I can't stop myself. When I was a child, excess was never pointed out to me as a failing – that was no doubt an error – but ever since then, I've been striding through literature like a field, where my footsteps flatten the grass for a moment, just long enough to see the path I've taken, and the immensity of what is yet to be discovered. This is what I do. This is my occupation. I read books, and I write books, they're just different. I sometimes have the impression that mine are like wooden cabins in the forest, old-fashioned, meticulous constructions, sanded boards and nails, lost in the middle of wide, wild spaces, a bit too solid to be truly beautiful. My books lack the intelligence, the glass-and-metal purity of modern prose, its subtleties of language, they betray my extreme caution, my respect of the status quo, my limitations, my smallness, because prose is perhaps the most intense and honest relationship I can have with the world around me and there's no other way I can go about it. Now that I think of it, calmly, for the first time, I can remember one of my mother's brothers, that Christmas when he gave their father an exorbitantly expensive electric rotary hoe, chosen with great care and for which he had no doubt worked hours of overtime collecting shellfish with a snorkel in the icy autumn seas – a literally stupefying gift laid under the folding plastic Christmas tree in the rickety house where we gathered near Lorient, and no one in the clan could understand how or even why he had gone to all that trouble for a father he would avoid when he saw him at the village café. *He has a sore back*, he finally admitted through clenched teeth – a piece of information that he was the only one to have guessed, and that left every single one of the rest of us mute. But my grandfather never used the thing, despite multiple desperate attempts by my uncle, who ended up tilling the garden himself, to the grumbling of his irascible father who told him he wasn't *doing the corners properly.* It was enough to break your heart. It took me a long time to understand what my mother told me that day as we watched them quarrelling in the vegetable garden. *My father just can't*, she explained while eating a plum. *He's a man of wood, of earth, of leaves. Not electricity or metal. He just* can't *use it. It's not his material. That's all.*

And so sometimes I remember that story when I'm thinking about my writing. I am not someone gifted with great visions. I'm only relatively intelligent, not very stable, and not at all subtle. I see words one by one, like stones, with which to build a cairn or an inuksuk, to find the only possible balance, to cast the most graceful line of ricochets between two riverbanks. My slowness is prodigious, I need to circle a book for years like an idiot before locating its heart, it's like carving a piece of wood with another piece of wood, but then it happens, all of a sudden, and it's wonderful. Grammar is my element, the clear water I swim in, my algebra, my only science, I've been writing so excessively and for so long, I guess I've missed out on a number of essential things but, within the magical and implacable laws of grammar, I practise my skills unto exhaustion, with great joy, as if I were locked up forever inside a squash court. As ridiculous as this may be, I've been writing for twenty-five years, trying to write books. Now that they're published, people believe, quite legitimately, that all is well – but I think they've forgotten what it was like before, when I was writing into the void, when I was blindly sacrificing huge things just to be alone and to write, at a time when my life held no meaning for anyone. Nowadays, of course, everything seems to have fallen into place – but I lived alone through years of fear that it never would, just as I'm still living alone dreading the years yet to come, about which I know nothing at all. Now that my books are on bookshop shelves and appear so logical, so obvious, they can serve to justify all my inadequacies, but I remember the time when my failings didn't yet have any explanation, when it was possible they never would, and I might be left forever standing outside the doors of what is important.

• *Julia Kerninon* was born in Nantes in 1987 and has a doctorate in American Literature. Her first novel, *Buvard*, has won many awards, including the Prix Françoise Sagan. She was granted a Lagardère young writer's scholarship in 2014. Her second novel, *Le dernier amour d'Attila Kiss*, won the Prix de la Closerie des Lilas in 2016. Her latest novel, *My Devotion*, won the 2018 Fénéon Literary Prize and is to be published in English by Europa Editions.

• *Ruth Diver* is the recipient of two French Voices Awards, as well as Asymptote's 2016 Close Approximations fiction prize. Her recent translations include the alexandrine verse in *The Reader on the 6.27* by Jean-Paul Didierlaurent, translated by Ros Schwartz, and Adélaïde Bon's *The Little Girl on the Ice Floe*.

Founded in 2014, Les Fugitives is an independent literary press that publishes contemporary francophone writers of fiction, non-fiction and everything in between, with an emphasis on first English translations of works by authors previously unpublished in the UK.

• Published by Les Fugitives:

• 2015 •

Nathalie Léger, *Suite for Barbara Loden*, trans. Natasha Lehrer and Cécile Menon.

• 2016 •

Ananda Devi, *Eve out of Her Ruins*, trans. Jeffrey Zuckerman (co-published with CB editions)

• 2017 •

Noémi Lefebvre, *Blue Self-Portrait*, trans. Sophie Lewis.

Mireille Gansel, *Translation as Transhumance*, trans. Ros Schwartz, with a foreword by Lauren Elkin.

• 2018 •

Jean Frémon, *Now, Now, Louison*, trans. Cole Swensen.

• 2019 •

Anne Serre, *The Governesses*, trans. Mark Hutchinson.

Sylvie Weil, *Selfies*, trans. Ros Schwartz.

Colette Fellous, *This Tilting World*, trans. Sophie Lewis, with a foreword by Michèle Roberts.

Nathalie Léger, *Exposition*, trans. Amanda DeMarco.

• 2020 •

Ananda Devi, *The Living Days*, trans. Jeffrey Zuckerman.

Nathalie Léger, *The White Dress*, trans. Natasha Lehrer.

Camille Laurens, *Little Dancer Aged Fourteen*, trans. Willard Wood.

Julia Kerninon, *A Respectable Occupation*, trans. Ruth Diver, with a foreword by Lauren Elkin.

Jean Frémon, *Nativity* (with original drawings by Louise Bourgeois), trans. Cole Swensen.